Willow
Finds a Way

In memory of the incredible Katie Darby, and for the girls who will always believe — L.B.

For my little boy, Finch, who napped just often enough for me to finish these pictures — T.H.

Kids Can Press acknowledges the financial support of the Government of Ontario, through the Ontario Media Development Corporation's Ontario Book Initiative; the Ontario Arts Council; the Canada Council for the Arts; and the Government of Canada, through the CBF, for our publishing activity.

Published in Canada by
Kids Can Press Ltd.
25 Dockside Drive
Toronto, ON M5A 0B5

Published in the U.S. by
Kids Can Press Ltd.
2250 Military Road
Tonawanda, NY 14150

www.kidscanpress.com

Kids Can Press is a **CORUS**™ Entertainment company

The artwork in this book was rendered in Photoshop. The text is set in Univers 45 and Bodoni.

Edited by Yvette Ghione and Debbie Rogosin
Designed by Karen Powers and Marie Bartholomew

This book is smyth sewn casebound.
Manufactured in Shen Zhen, Guang Dong, P.R. China, in 09/2012 by Printplus Limited

CM 13 0 9 8 7 6 5 4 3 2 1

Library and Archives Canada Cataloguing in Publication

Button, Lana, 1968–
    Willow finds a way / written by Lana Button ; illustrated by Tania Howells.

ISBN 978-1-55453-842-3

1. Bullying in schools — Juvenile fiction. I. Howells, Tania II. Title.

PS8603.U87W45 2013   jC813'.6   C2012-904801-1

Willow Finds a Way

Written by Lana Button Illustrated by Tania Howells

KIDS CAN PRESS

IN Willow's class, Kristabelle was the boss.
Willow wished for words that would say,
"*no,*" when Kristabelle told her where to sit,
and what to play, and who to play with.
But when Kristabelle spoke, *everyone* did
as they were told. Even Willow.

One morning, Kristabelle skipped into the classroom holding
a pink sparkly paper. "*I* am having a *fantastic* birthday party!"
she announced. "You can come," she said, holding the paper high,
"*if* you are on my birthday list!"

Willow joined the crowd around Kristabelle. She saw …

Jane
Tianna
Julian

Her heart thumped so loudly, Willow was sure the whole class could hear it beating. *Please let my name be there,* she thought.

Mateo
Leena
Olivia
Juan

When her eyes reached the bottom of the list, she was almost too scared to look. But then she read the last name on the pink sparkly paper … and she beamed.

Willow

Everyone was invited!

At snack time, Kristabelle waved the birthday list in the air and said,
"*If* you want to stay on my birthday list, come sit at *my* table!"

Willow was comfortable where she was. But then Julian moved.
And so did Jane.

Willow worried she wouldn't be part of the fantastic birthday party, so …
she squished in as well.

At playtime, Willow and Jane were busy in the sandbox when Kristabelle waved the birthday list again and said, "Everyone on my birthday list, come play with *me* on the climber!"

Willow was happy playing in the sand. But then Jane rushed right overtop of their castle calling, "Let's go, Willow!"

Willow worried that she wouldn't be part of the fantastic birthday party, so … she stood at the climber with everyone else and clapped for Kristabelle.

At the end of the day, Kristabelle walked
straight to the front of the line holding tight
to her birthday list.

   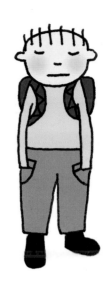

Mateo took a brave step ahead of her and smiled. "Remember, Kristabelle? Mrs. Post said it's my turn to be Line Leader."

"But, Mateo," Kristabelle said in an angry whisper that was just loud enough that Mrs. Post wouldn't hear, "*I* am having a fantastic birthday party, so *I* should be Line Leader!"

Mateo stood firmly in his spot. "Sorry, Kristabelle. I really want my turn."

"Fine!" said Kristabelle, stamping her foot, "*You* are not my friend anymore and …"

"You can't come to my birthday party!"

Everyone watched as Kristabelle held up the birthday list and drew a line straight through Mateo's name.

Mateo's lip trembled. Willow took a deep breath to say, "That's not nice, Kristabelle." But nothing came out.

"Wear pink tomorrow!" Kristabelle called as everyone went out the door. "Pink is my favorite color. So wear pink if you want to come to my *fantastic* birthday party!"

The next morning as she got ready for school,
Willow searched for words to say to Kristabelle.
But her head swirled with visions of parties and
pink sparkly lists … and a line drawn straight
through *her* name.

So, instead, Willow searched her drawers
for pink things to wear.

At snack time, Willow trailed behind the crowd to Kristabelle's table. "Oh, Willow, I love your dress!" Kristabelle said sweetly. Willow was relieved.

Then Kristabelle turned to Julian. "Where is *your* pink?" she asked.

"I don't like pink," said Julian.

Kristabelle got out her marker and drew a line through Julian's name. "You can't come to my birthday party!" she said.

Julian grabbed his snack and stomped over to the table where Mateo was sitting alone.

Jane looked down at the floor. Tianna fidgeted in her seat. Willow struggled to say, "Kristabelle, that's mean!" But the words just wouldn't come out.

Again Willow's head swirled with visions of parties and pink sparkly lists … and a line drawn straight through *her* name!

Then Willow knew just what to do.

Without saying a word, she picked up Kristabelle's birthday list and a marker. She drew a line straight through her *own* name.

The whole class gasped. And at first, no one moved. But then Jane walked over and slowly took the birthday list from Willow's hands.

One by one, everyone crossed their names off Kristabelle's birthday list.
Just like that, Kristabelle wasn't the boss of anyone!

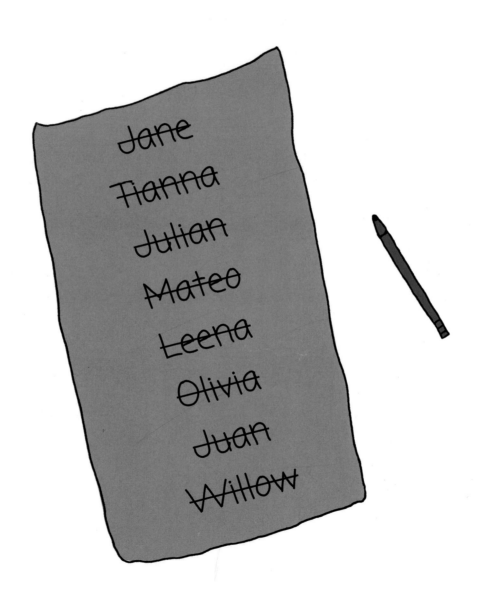

So Kristabelle sat all by herself at snack time.

Willow was happy to be in her regular spot. But she noticed that Kristabelle didn't eat a thing.

At playtime, Willow tried to concentrate on her sand castle, but she could see Kristabelle all alone on the climber. Kristabelle did some pretty impressive tricks. But no one clapped.

At the end of the day, everyone rushed into line, so Kristabelle had to go to the very end.

Jane saved a spot for Willow right in the middle. But Willow went to the back of the line instead … to stand with Kristabelle.

At first Kristabelle was surprised. But then she
looked down at the floor. "I'm sorry," she said,
in a voice that was just loud enough for Willow
to hear.

Before Willow could say a word, Kristabelle marched straight over to Mrs. Post. Everyone watched uneasily as Kristabelle whispered in her ear.

"Oh, my," Mrs. Post said as Kristabelle pointed to the line of children.

"Hmmm," said Mrs. Post, when Kristabelle was finished. Mrs. Post addressed the class with her hands on her hips. "Boys and girls." Everyone held their breath. "Kristabelle would like to make an announcement."

"My birthday party will be fantastic," Kristabelle said, holding the birthday list up high. And then, to everyone's surprise, she ripped it into pink sparkly pieces. "If *all* of my friends will come ... *please*?"

And they did! And *everyone* had a wonderful time.